D1347610

SUPER
DOOPER
JEZEBEL

Tony Ross

For Jan and Paul

First published in Great Britain by Andersen Press Ltd in 1988
First published in Picture Lions in 1989
This edition published in 1993
Picture Lions is an imprint of the Children's Division,
part of HarperCollins Publishers Limited,
77-85 Fulham Palace Road, Hammersmith,
London W6 8JB

Printed in Great Britain by BPCC Paulton Books

SUPER DOOPER JEZEBEL

Tony Ross

PictureLions

An Imprint of HarperCollinsPublishers

Jezebel was perfect in every way. She was so perfect
she was called Super Dooper Jezebel.

When other children came out of school, they were
sometimes untidy.

but Jezebel was always super dooper neat.

Jezebel always kept her room tidy, and she always put her things back in their boxes . . .

and she cleaned up after the cat.

When she went out to play with her friends,

Jezebel always kept clean. (She still liked to have two baths every day.)

She always wrote her "thank you" letters, in neat
writing, without being reminded,

and at school, she was best at everything.

When she had spots, she always took her medicine
(and said, "Thank you.")

She could do up buttons, and tie real bows on her lace-ups.

Jezebel always ate up her meals. She always put
her knife and fork together,

and she *never* picked her nose.

Jezebel told other children not to do things . . .

because it was nice being perfect.

When the Prime Minister heard about Jezebel,
she sent her a special medal for being good,

and a special statue of Jezebel was put up in the park, to remind everybody else to try to be perfect.

She even went on television, in a special show
to talk about herself and her medal,

and the cups she had won for being polite, being
spotless, being helpful, being best at sums, reading,
poetry and writing.

At school, Super Dooper Jezebel wouldn't do *anything* wrong . . .

like the other noisy children who weren't perfect . . .

CLUMP!

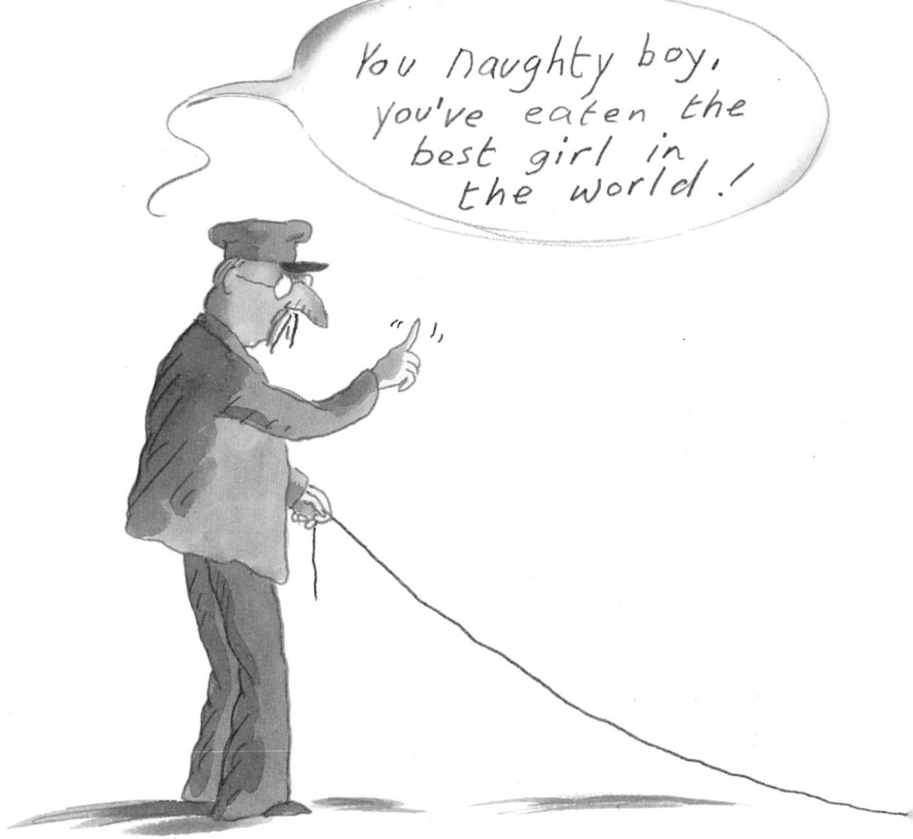
You naughty boy, you've eaten the best girl in the world!

Tony Ross was born in London in 1938. His dream was to work with horses but instead he went to art college in Liverpool. Since then, Tony has worked as an art director at an advertising agency, a graphic designer, a cartoonist, a teacher and a film maker – as well as illustrating over 150 books! Tony and his wife Zoë live in Macclesfield, Cheshire and have four children.

Picture Lions by Tony Ross
I WANT MY POTTY
THE KNIGHT WHO WAS AFRAID OF THE DARK
JENNA AND THE TROUBLEMAKER